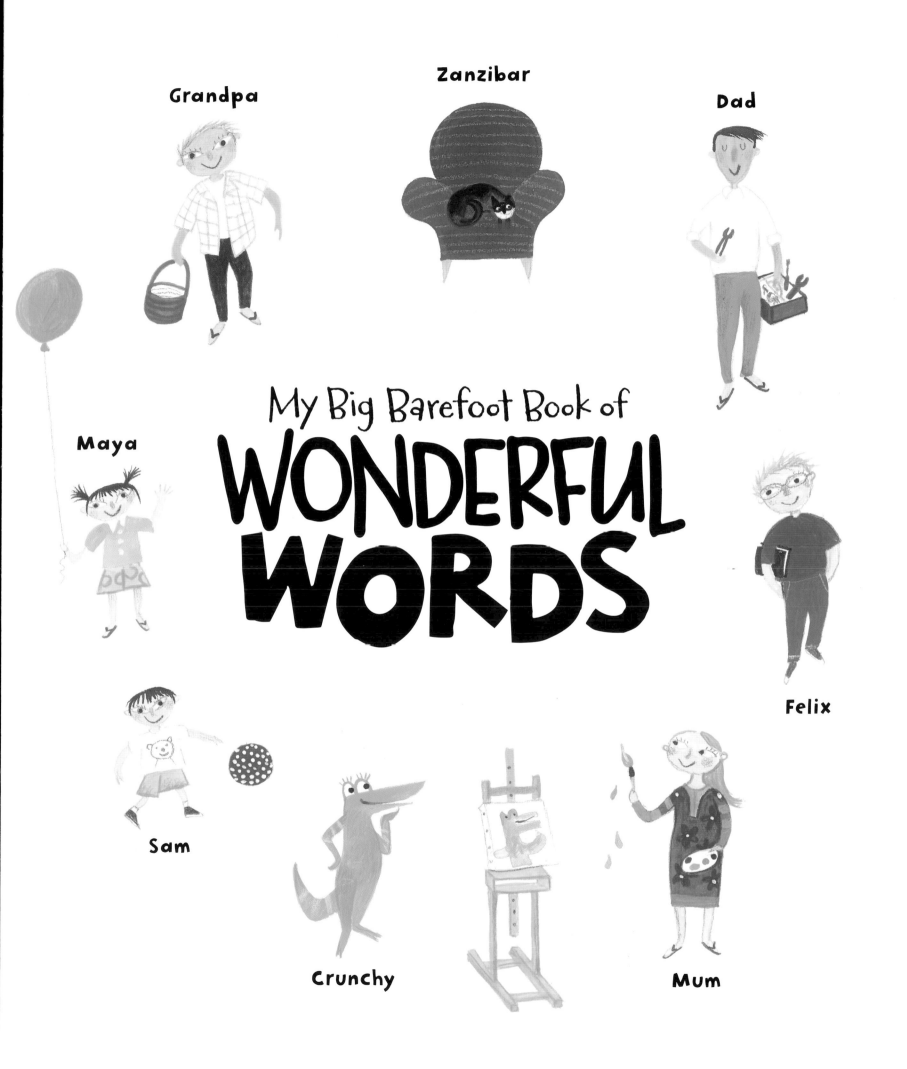

Grandpa

Zanzibar

Dad

Maya

My Big Barefoot Book of
WONDERFUL
WORDS

Felix

Sam

Crunchy

Mum

For my family:
Nick, Sasha, Darrin
and Pammy Jane
— K. M. J. D.

For Anna Andrisani,
Antonio Amato, Mara,
Palma, Carmen and Enzo,
such a wonderful family!
— S. F.

Barefoot Books
294 Banbury Road
Oxford, OX2 7ED

Text copyright © 2014 by Barefoot Books
Illustrations copyright © 2014 by Sophie Fatus
The moral rights of Barefoot Books
and Sophie Fatus have been asserted

First published in Great Britain
by Barefoot Books, Ltd in 2014
All rights reserved

Graphic design by Katie Jennings Campbell,
Asheville, North Carolina, USA
Reproduction by B & P International, Hong Kong
Printed in China on 100% acid-free paper
This book was typeset in Slappy
The illustrations were prepared in
mixed media: acrylic and coloured pencils

ISBN 978-1-78285-091-5

British Cataloguing-in-Publication Data:
a catalogue record of this book is
available from the British Library

1 3 5 7 9 8 6 4 2

My Big Barefoot Book of

WONDERFUL
WORDS

Sophie Fatus

Barefoot Books
step inside a story

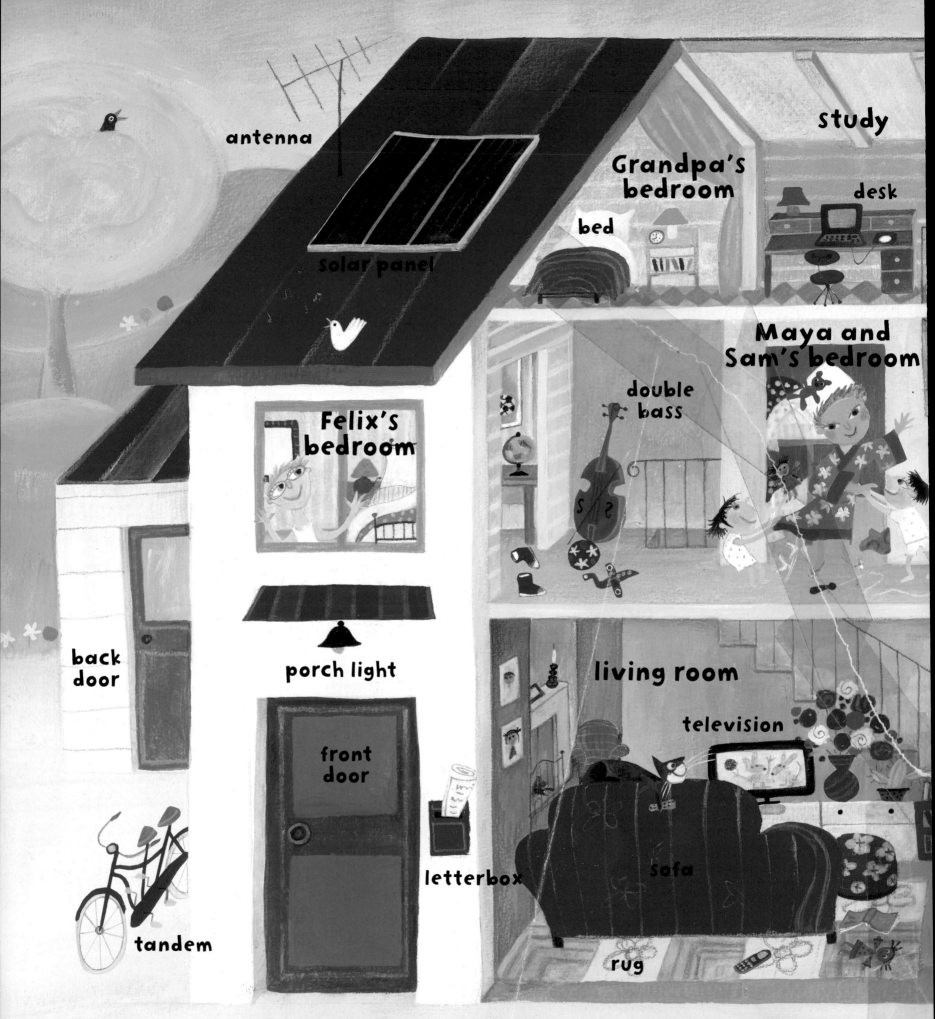

antenna

study

Grandpa's bedroom

bed

desk

solar panel

Maya and Sam's bedroom

Felix's bedroom

double bass

back door

porch light

living room

television

front door

letterbox

sofa

tandem

rug

It's morning time at our house.
The birds are chirping.

ceiling

roof

corridor

exercise
bike

window

toilet

wall

Mum and
Dad's bedroom

mirror

double
bed

sink

stairs

bathroom

shower

landing

picture

dining room

light

bookcase

table

chairs

wool
basket

floor

kitchen

Wake up, everyone!

Let's get dressed!

baseball cap

orange cardigan

sarong

mitten missing its mate

red t-shirt

white vest

cowboy hat

boxer shorts

trousers

yellow raincoat

trainers

pink party dress

cat

dashiki

tartan kilt

beret

What would you like to wear today?

purple kimono

straw hat

stripy tights

gloves

fuzzy earmuffs

grey tracksuit

socks

shorts

blouse

skirt

blue dungarees

sandals

salwar kameez

green tunic

sari

brown boots

black shoes

mugs

cupboard

biscuit tin

plates

fruit basket

blender

eggs

fridge

knife

milk

tagine

pickles

sink

bowl

chopping board

juice

dishwasher

bins

drawer

spatula

jam

teapot

Everyone is making breakfast. The hot chocolate smells delicious.

Don't let Crunchy eat the pancakes!

stockpot

hot chocolate

pan

bacon

hob

frying pan

oven

rocket pancakes

spoon

fork

sugar bowl

table

orange juice

cereal

whisk

mixing bowl

measuring spoons

bread

butter

toaster

burnt toast

tiles

After breakfast, Mum and Dad go to the workshop.

tomato chutney

pins

wall

mannequin

preserving jars

axe

handsaw

fabric bolt

wrench

toolbox

apron

hammer

rag

nails

spool

scissors

paint

palette

workbench

paintbrushes

measuring tape

Dad's old photo albums

tins of paint

paint roller

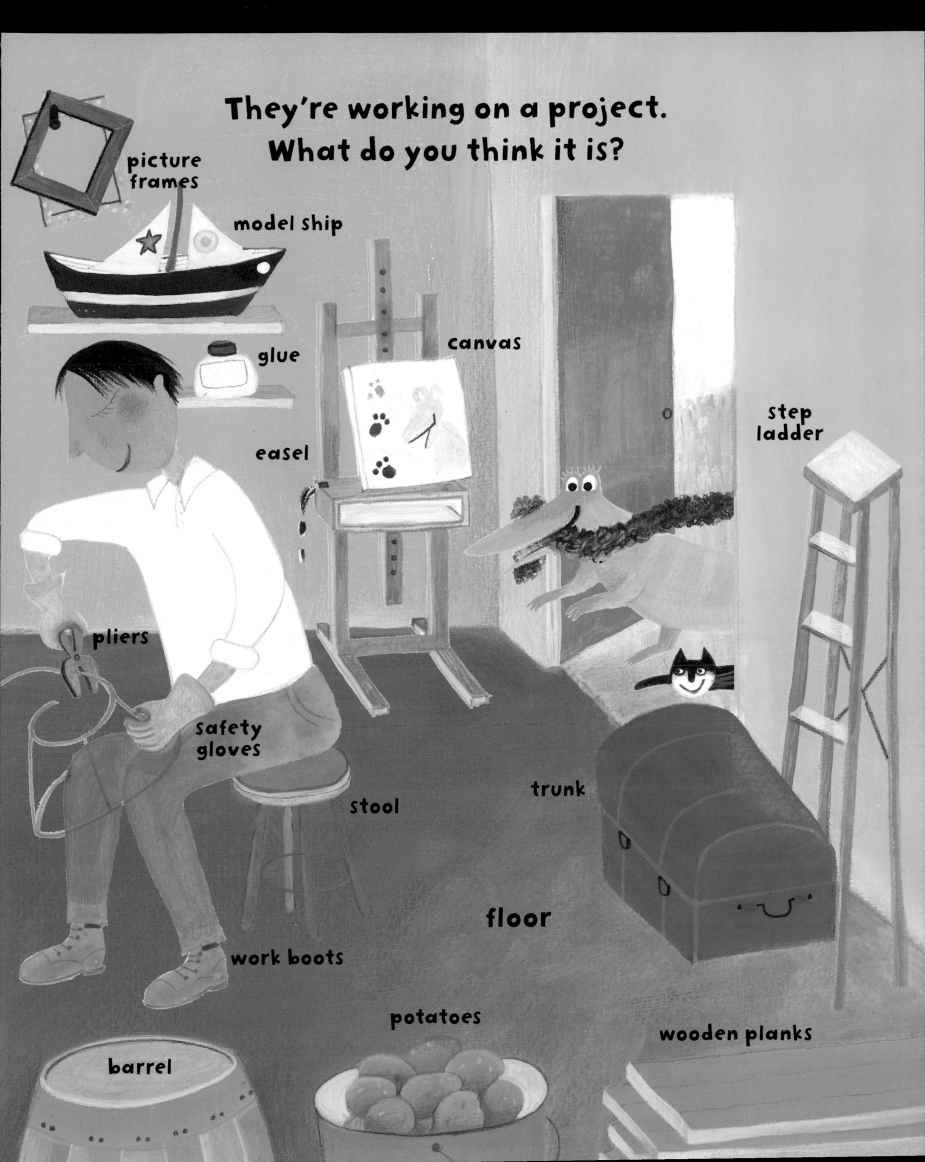

Grandpa is reading his newspaper in the garden.

vegetable patch

courgettes

chicken coop

tomato plants

tomato plants

beehive

Mavis, Beatrice, Matilda and Lara

pea plants

shoots

seeds

spade

path

lettuces

wheelbarrow

hose pipe

hoe

garden fork

fence

wire

arm bands

paddling pool

water butt

rake

lawn mower

logs

recycling bin

compost bin

rubbish bin

trellis

'Grandpa, will you take us to the library, please?' asks Sam.

ladybird

butterfly

washing line

tree

clothes pegs

tyre swing

lawn

newspaper

garden chair

bush

'And then can we go to the park?' asks Maya.

carrot

potato

turnip

beetroot

Brussels sprouts

spinach

green beans

tomatoes

garden peas

squash

broccoli

sweetcorn

cauliflower

lettuce

'Of course!' says Grandpa. 'Let's go to town.
But first, let's pick some vegetables.'

It's a sunny day. The streets are busy.

bicycle shop

bookshop

farmers' market

toy shop

Chinese restaurant

fire station

computer repair shop

chemist

library

kitchen shop

hairdresser

dentist

community centre

clothes shop

hotel

café

art gallery

police station

florist

doctor's surgery

vet

sushi bar

bakery

greengrocer

delicatessen

bistro

post office

Look at all these people!

artist

musician

construction worker

writer

editor

architect

farmer

teacher

photographer

bookseller

doctor

carpenter

football player

chef

police officer

astronaut

Sam wants to be a chef.

acrobat

ballet dancer

firefighter

vet

mechanic

judge

reporter

bus driver

actor

tree surgeon

potter

hairdresser

fashion designer

What do you want to be when you grow up?

Look! It's a building site.

crane

forklift truck

bulldozer

safety cones

sandbags

pneumatic drill

architect

foreman

architect's plans

buckets

set square

scaffolding

Grandpa says they're
building a new house here.

What kind of home would you like to live in?

castle

houseboat

mansion

igloo

stilt house

tree house

croft

bell tent

town house

caravan

tepee

block of flats

A-frame

roundhouse

palace

thatched cottage

terraced house

farmhouse

eco house

cave

geodesic dome

log cabin

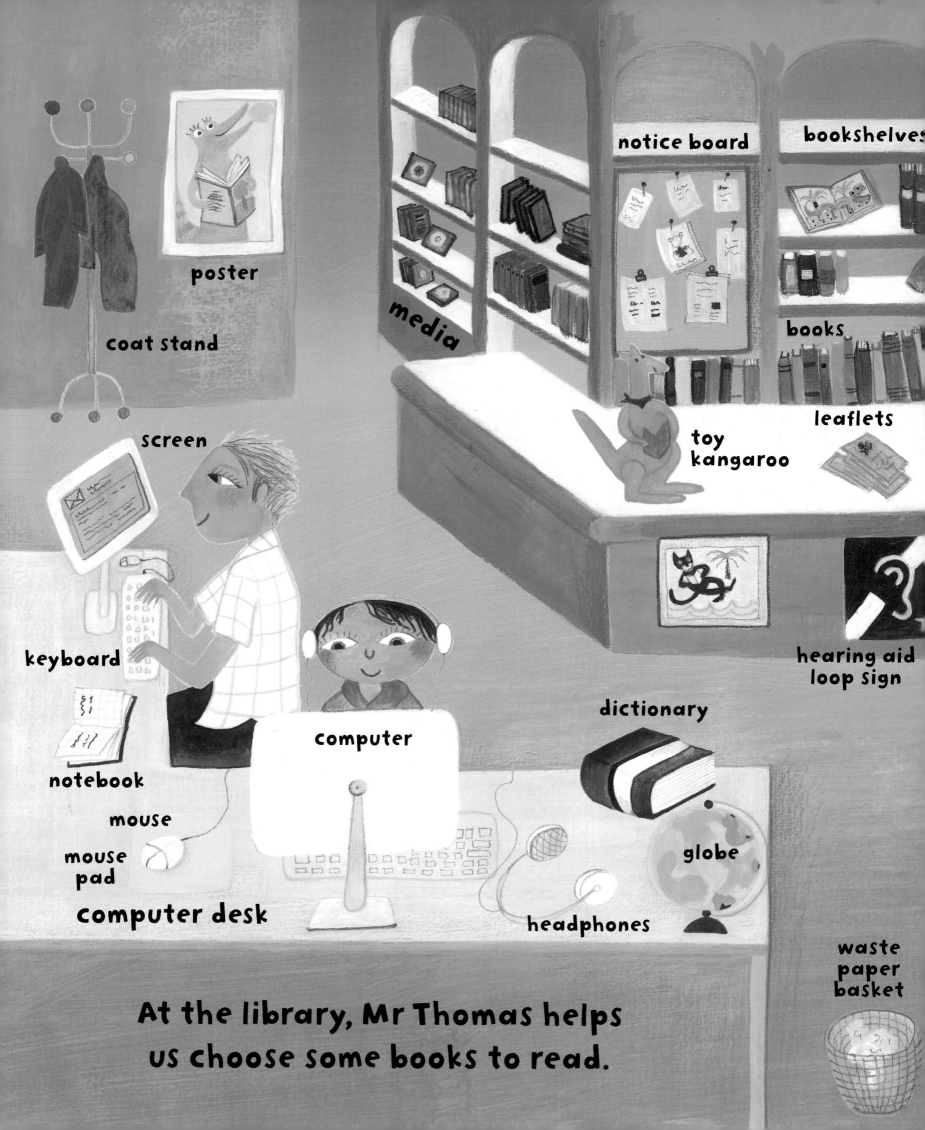

poster

coat stand

media

notice board

bookshelves

books

toy kangaroo

leaflets

screen

keyboard

hearing aid loop sign

notebook

dictionary

computer

mouse

globe

mouse pad

computer desk

headphones

waste paper basket

At the library, Mr Thomas helps us choose some books to read.

bookcases

lost property box

librarian

magazines

rubber stamp

counter

book return

origami bird

paper boat

Braille book

scissors

pencil crayons

pipe cleaners

stickers

paper plates

craft tables

Sam likes stories with
lots of magic in them.

Which story characters would you like to meet?

angel

warrior

alien

fairy

prince

elf

giant

griffin

dragon

goblin

knight

ghost

princess

troll

vampire

queen

king

spy

witch

burglar

wizard

mermaid

unicorn

At the market, Grandpa
buys a jar of golden honey.
'This looks like a good one,' he says.

meat

pork

books

mushrooms

herbs

spices

Cheddar

Gouda

Roquefort

Brie

goat's cheese

cheese

eggs

mozzarella

twine

meat cleaver

steak

lamb

beef

butcher's block

waxed paper

baguettes

sweets

fruit

weighing scales

oranges

apples

grapes

kiwi fruit

bananas

pineapples

poultry

hens

duck

roses

carnations

flowers

wreath

tulips

sunflowers

daisies

lavender

After the market, we go to the park.

kite

bench

sand pit

walking frame

football

bubbles

marbles

slide

playground

roller skates

It's full of children playing. Let's join in!

sandwich

ants

forward roll

carrots

lemonade

picnic basket

thermos flask

hummus

biscuits

picnic rug

skateboard

seesaw

skipping rope

grass

rope swing

hopscotch

swing

Everyone in the park looks happy and relaxed.

sad

bored

impatient

embarrassed

puzzled

calm

angry

thoughtful

offended

jealous

disgusted

curious

annoyed

hungry

hopeful

sleepy

patient

nervous

happy

excited

scared

wary

loving

poorly

lonely

How do you think these children feel?

It's time to go home now.

signal

pavement

manhole

road

lollipop man

zebra crossing

lamppost

rickshaw

advertisement

flag

church

bus stop

BIKES

street
sign

mosque

café

postbox

taxi stand

pedestrian

paper
boy

newsagent

temple

bike rack

Look—our bus is coming. Hurry!

There are so many ways to get around.

rocket

van

glider

roller skates

car

dinghy

helicopter

hot air balloon

hiking boots

underground train

scooter

horse

How do you like to travel?

barge

train

rowing boat

vintage sports car

aeroplane

motorcycle

skateboards

lorry

bicycle

fire engine

police car

bus

We leave the town and drive
through the countryside.

As we make our way home,
big raindrops begin to fall.

It looks like there's going to be a thunderstorm!

clouds

fog

hail

ice

barometer

drizzle

sleet

tornado

umbrella

wind sock

What is your favourite kind of weather?

 rain

 frost

hurricane

sun

snow

weather vane

 rainbow

thunderstorm

blizzard  wind

lightning

A rainy night is perfect for spending time together.

Where is the missing puzzle piece?

painting

candle

mirror

photograph

logs

fireplace

bellows

chess

cushion

lamp shade

light bulb

playing cards

armchair

Maya's book is all about animals.

dog

yak

buffalo

xoona moth

elephant

umbrella bird

wolf

anteater

quail

parrot

giraffe

meerkat

nightingale

snake

Which animal would you like to have as a pet?
Can you put the animals in alphabetical order?

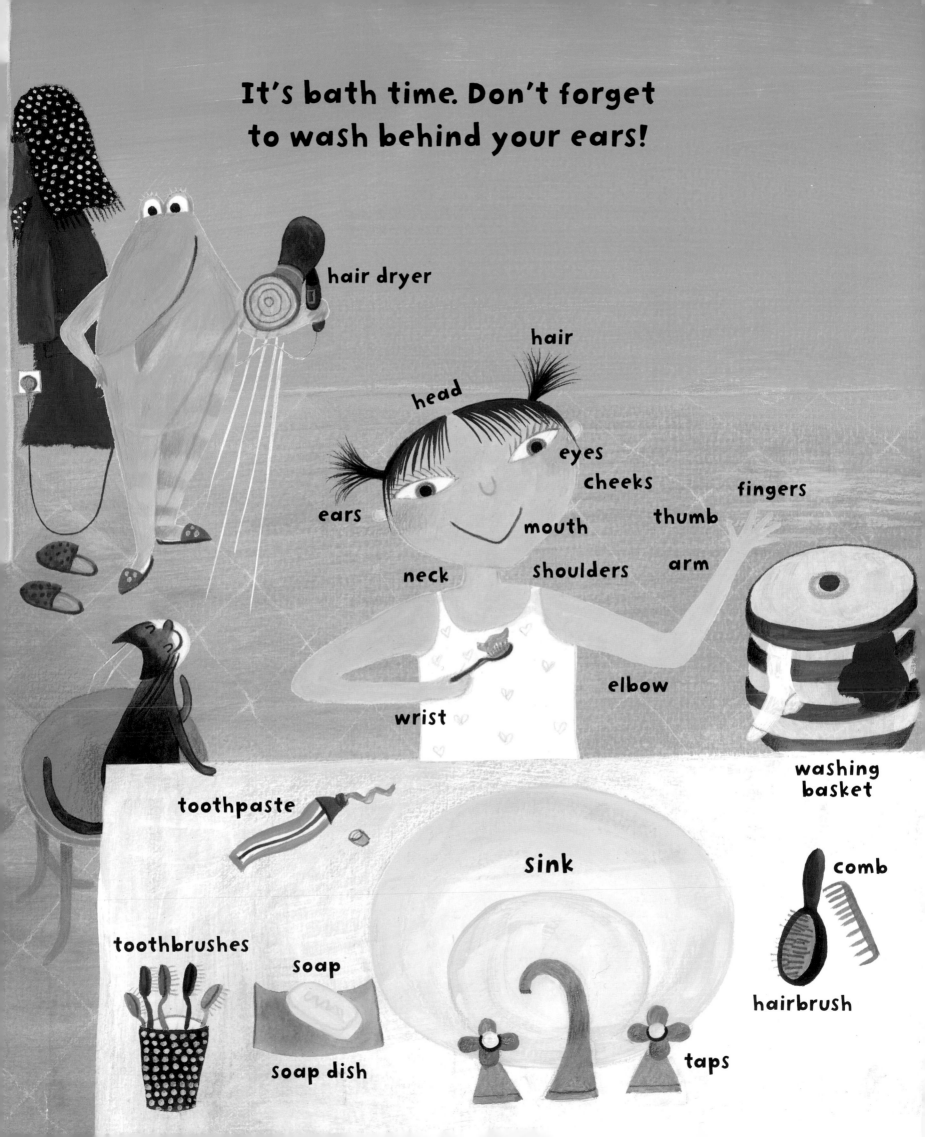

It's time to go to bed.
Night night! Sleep tight!